TW HOOTS

In memory of Bert

Feeder of bird
Feeder of squirrel

First published in the USA 2017 by Roaring Brook Press
First published in the UK 2017 by Two Hoots
This edition published 2018 by Two Hoots
an imprint of Pan Macmillan
20 New Wharf Road, London N1 9RR
Associated companies throughout the world
www.panmacmillan.com
ISBN 978-1-5098-4056-4
Text and illustrations copyright © Lane Smith 2017
Moral rights asserted.

9 8 7 6 5 4 3 2 1
A CIP catalogue record for this book is available from the British Library.
Printed in China

The illustrations in this book were created with oil paints over a gesso surface.
Also used were acrylic varnish spray, pen and ink, coloured pencil and digital
cut and paste.

www.twohootsbooks.com

The warmth of the sun . . .

felt good on Cat's back.

Cat liked to be in
the flower bed where
the daffodils grew.

It was a perfect day for Cat.

The cool of the
water was what
Dog liked best.

When it was hot,
Dog sat in the
wading pool that
his friend Bert
filled for him.

It was a perfect day for Dog.

Birdseed.

Bert topped up the bird feeder with it.

It was a perfect day for Bird.

Squirrel went up
the pole.

Squirrel went
down the pole.

Squirrel could not
get to the seed.

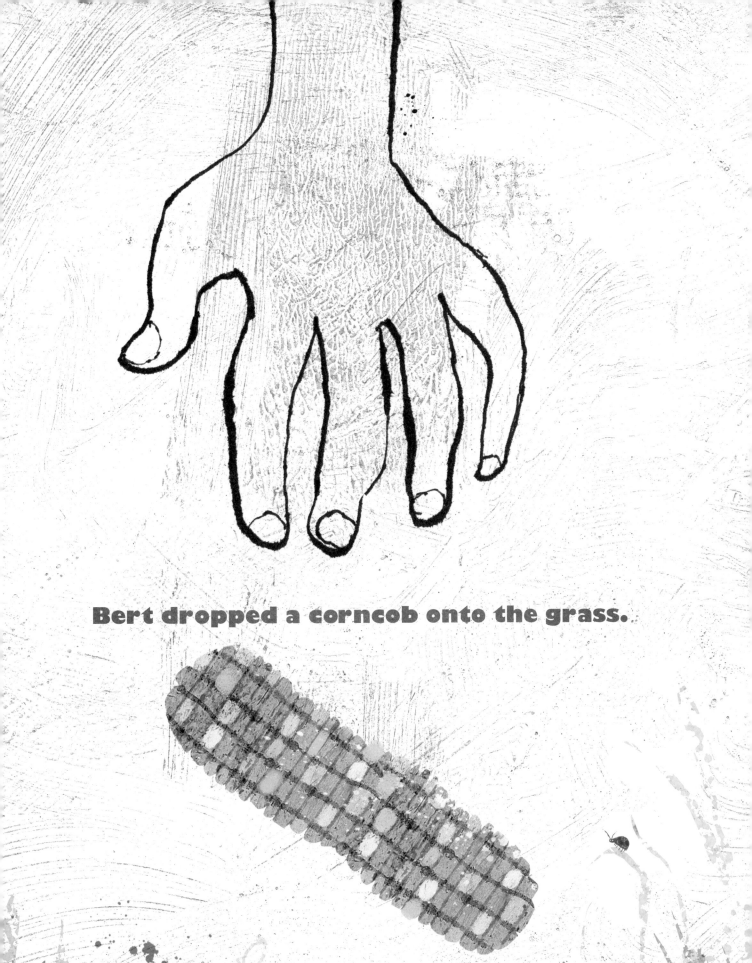

Bert dropped a corncob onto the grass.

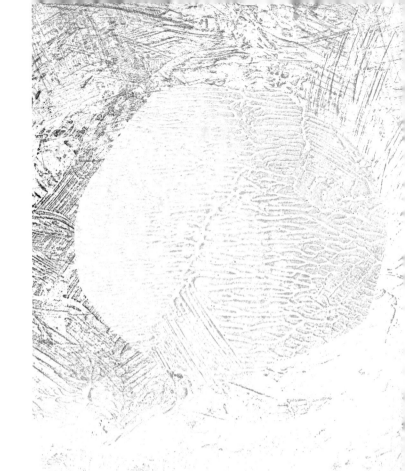

It was a perfect day for Squirrel.

It **was** a perfect day for Squirrel.

It **was** a perfect day for Bird.

It **was** a perfect day for Dog.

It **was** a perfect day for Cat.

The warmth of the sun.
The cool of the water.
A belly full of corn and seed.
A flower bed for a nap.

It was a perfect day for Bear.